I'LL REMEMBER

a screenplay-novel
by

Clif Mc Crady

Aignos Publishing
an imprint of Savant Books and Publications
Honolulu, HI, USA
2019

Published in the USA by Aignos Publishing LLC
An imprint of Savant Books and Publications LLC
2630 Kapiolani Blvd #1601
Honolulu, HI 96826
http://www.savantbooksandpublications.com

Printed in the USA

Edited by Eleonor Gardner
Cover by Daniel S. Janik
Cover images: "Old man veteran viewing map with grandson showing
front line, remembering war " ID 132356347 © motortion |
Dreamstime.com and "Hall of Names in the Yad Vashem Holocaust
Memorial Site in Jerusalem, Israel" ID 145038020 © Brasilnut |
Dreamstime.com

13 digit ISBN: 9780999463369

First Edition: December 2019
Library of Congress Control Number: 2019953738

Dedication

Dedicated to my grandparents, as well as librarians all over the world.

Acknowledgements

To those who lived and died during the Holocaust and our World War II veterans who inspired this story; Stage III Community Theatre; and Herbert Hoover Jr. High School.

Foreword
Permission Information & Playwright Notes

The following requirements are for all public performances or uses of the play (even if admission is not charged):

1. All programs, posters, other publicity for the play etc. should have the author's name (Clif Mc Crady) printed on them, roughly half the size of the title of the play.

2. Please Credit Stage III Community Theatre as the original producer of the play. Visit www.stageiiitheatre.org for more information.

3. When a production is completed, please mail a copy of the production's program to: Clif Mc Crady, P.O. Box 853, Casper, WY 82602.

4. Some playwrights are tied to gender--I am not. I view theatre as a collaborative art. In my mind, the writer, director and actors all work together to tell a story.

Maybe you feel a part would best be played by someone of the opposite gender. Yes, "Grandpa" would best be played by an older man, but I say, let's collaborate. Maybe your vision and casting of a woman to play "Grandpa" would result in choosing the right actor; maybe she could play him better. Also, some of the parts written for a male or female can be played by anyone. For example, "Bob the Bartender" may just as easily be "Barb the Bartender" as long as you change the pronouns. I can work with this type of change. As long as I am alive, we can always discuss alternate versions or adaptations. However, any changes as such, would become property of the playwright.

5. **Royalty Rates**. The publisher shall have sole discretion in determining commercially-reasonable royalty fees, with the exception that a standard royalty of any amount less than $25 per performance (please check for any change of rate) of the play, shall be subject to the playwright's written approval. This approval shall not be unreasonably withheld.

6. **Production rights**. Unless otherwise mutually noted between play producers, no other performances shall be scheduled within an agreed upon geographic area (how about a 50-mile radius to start with?). Also, the play's production should either open or close within 90 days of a performance run.

So, if you choose to run my play in Sacramento, California, with opening night on August 1 and closing night August 15, then we (or another playhouse) won't schedule another playhouse in the region. Instead, a presentation would be scheduled say in Roseville, California, and not until after November 15. Chico (about 100+

miles from Sacramento) would not be so restricted.

Again, we can come to a collaborative agreement in this regard. This may also cause a delay in production rights if the theatre is unable to perform in their agreed-on performance window. Notable exceptions would be high schools.

7. **Optional but appreciated.** I hope you will agree to be a resource for future producers of this play. If so, I will have your name, mailing address and/or email address available for future reference.

Thank you for selecting my script. I hope you enjoy it.

- Clif Mc Crady

The Original Cast from the First Production at Stage III Community Theatre in Casper, Wyoming

from April 26, 2013 to May 11, 2013

Role	Actor
Lisa Talbot	Nicole Collier
Narrator Jim Talbot	Jim Gunderson
Ms. Linda Douglas	Lindsay Gustafson
Jimmy Talbot	Gabe Stanley

Clif Mc Crady

Joan Talbot (Mom)	Julia Sabo
Grandpa Jerome Talbot	Rob Oldham
Anton Gregorovich	Clint Saunders
Anne Frank	Emily DiVita
Helmut Dreizinger	Sterling Harvell
Sarah Stein	Sharon Roberts-Meyer

I'll Remember

I'll
Remember

By
Clif Mc Crady

Cast of Characters

LISA TALBOT—Mid-30's daughter of the play's narrator, Grown-up Jim Talbot.

NARRATOR (JIM TALBOT)—Mid-60's father of Lisa Talbot, son of Joan Talbot and grandson of Grandpa Jerome Talbot.

JIMMY TALBOT—13 years old.

MS. LINDA DOUGLAS—Early 30's junior high school librarian.

GRANDPA JEROME TALBOT—Mid-60's grandfather of Jimmy Talbot.

JOAN "MOM" TALBOT mid-40's mother of Jimmy Talbot.

ANTON GREGOROVICH—Mid-40's to mid-50's Russian Chess Master

ANNE FRANK—Based on the historic character; 13-15 years old.

HELMUT DREIZINGER—Mid to late 20-year-old.

SARAH STEIN—Late 50's.

```
Act I

Prologue            Narrator Jim Talbot's Library
Act I, Scene 1              School Library
Act I, Scene 2            Jimmy's Bedroom
Act I, Scene 3            Jimmy's Bedroom
Act I, Scene 4              School Library
Act I, Scene 5            Jimmy's Bedroom
Act I, Scene 6              School Library
Act I, Scene 7            Jimmy's Bedroom
Act I, Scene 8              School Library


Act II

Act II, Scene 1            Jimmy's Bedroom
Act II, Scene 2              School Library
Act II, Scene 3            Jimmy's Bedroom
Act II, Scene 4            Jimmy's Bedroom
Act II, Scene 5              School Library
Act II, Scene 6              School Library
Act II, Scene 7              School Library
Epilogue            Narrator Jim Talbot's Library
```

Prologue

At curtain rise, Lisa sits in a comfortable chair in her father's house. Next to her is a box of old photographs, letters, an old yearbook, and other memorabilia. She is looking through the box. She is obviously sad.

LISA:

Oh my. (*She pulls out an old beat-up copy of* The Diary of Anne Frank. *She looks at the book, then back inside the box.*) What's this? (*She pulls out another book. There is no name on this book. She opens it.*) Dad wrote this? (*She starts to read through it.*)

(*Enter Narrator*)

LISA and NARRATOR:

I can't remember the day, or even what the weather was like...

NARRATOR:

...when I first saw her face or when I first fell in love with her. The only thing I can tell you, was that it was in the winter. Late January or early February to be more precise. The school librarian introduced us.

LISA:

(*Lisa closes the book.*) Can I read this? (*pauses*) I shouldn't. (*sets the book down*) But there might be something important in it. (*picks the book up again and opens it to where she left off.*)

NARRATOR:

I remember the very first time I looked in her eyes. I was pulled in. She was just about my age. It was like she and I were intertwined, destined in some way to touch each other's lives...or at least she was destined to touch mine.

LISA:

Ah, first love? (*smiles*)

NARRATOR:

I had been unable to attend any P.E. Classes for more than half a school year.

LISA:

He told me about that.

NARRATOR:

Two broken ankles and some kind of strange stomach ailment, that still has not been diagnosed, led to a lot of book reading.

I spent a lot of time in the library. But I couldn't really help shelve books or anything, so for that one hour when I was supposed to be in P.E., I was in the library, reading.

You may hear people say librarians aren't 'real teachers', or say something to the effect of, 'She's just the librarian,' but I tell you, Miz Douglas introduced me to the likes of J.R.R. Tolkien, Isaac Asimov, Ray Bradbury and others.

While sitting in the library, I was able to stand on Mount Olympus; fight the Trojans; and it was Ms. Douglas who first introduced me to Athos, Porthos and Aramis. She was the first person who allowed me to express myself with paint. *My* expression...not someone else's. (*reflective*) How much influence did that one woman have in my life? I will probably never be able to measure how much.

(*Lights out*)

ACT I, SCENE 1

Lights up. It's 1977, inside a junior high school library. Many books are stacked on shelves around the room. A few chess sets and big tables position about the room, tables that could easily seat eight people. Scattered about are a globe, maps, a card catalog, and a large selection of poster-sized pictures neatly arranged in a file system. Ms. Douglas sits at her desk reading a book. Narrator stands by the card catalog.

SFX: Beethoven's String Quartet opus no. 130 Cavatina is playing on a cassette recorder.

Enter Jimmy. He is 13 years old, and on crutches. He has a backpack that could easily be holding 20 or 30 pounds of books.

NARRATOR:

That winter day was like any other junior high school day really. Mostly unmemorable, but I remember some parts of it so very well.

JIMMY:

Hello, Miz Douglas. I finished the Hobbit
stories.

MS. DOUGLAS:

(*turns off music*) In a week? Are you sure you
didn't just skim them?

JIMMY:

No, ma'am. I read them. But I am ready for
something new.

MS. DOUGLAS:

What do you think you would like?

JIMMY:

I really don't want fantasy or science fiction
this time.

MS. DOUGLAS:

What then?

JIMMY:

I was thinking about something from World War Two. I found out my uncle--well, my mom's uncle anyway--was a pilot.

NARRATOR:

That was all I knew about my grandmother's baby brother. He was a pilot in World War Two. I didn't know what he flew or where he flew, just that he was a pilot.

MS. DOUGLAS:

Hmmm, let me go see what's in the card catalog. (*Jimmy and Ms. Douglas go to the card catalog.*)

NARRATOR:

Knowing this was my second broken leg in six months after a long illness, Miz Douglas was nicer to me than she was to most of the other kids who came into the library. She was very protective of the books.

MS. DOUGLAS:

I'm not seeing anything specifically about pilots in the war. We have a couple of books about the Battle of the Bulge. Hmmm. Montgomery in Africa, Patton, an Eisenhower biography...

NARRATOR:

She kept mentioning all those names. I had heard about President Eisenhower, but the rest of them--Patton, Montgomery, Bradley, Rommel, Nimitz, Halsey--all these I knew nothing about. I didn't realize till the end of the school year, how much I didn't know.

JIMMY:

(*with a wry look on his face*) Then, how about something about girls?

MS. DOUGLAS:

What is that for?

JIMMY:

Someday I might get to move without these crutches, and maybe get to go to a dance.

MS. DOUGLAS:

What about a book about a girl in World War Two?

JIMMY:

That would be cool.

MS. DOUGLAS:

(looking again in the card catalog) I have something that might be good for you.

NARRATOR:

There was one thing that sounded particularly good to me that year: Everything I couldn't do-- swimming, walking the dog, baseball,and, yes, girls. But after eight weeks of not being able to do anything, I would have enjoyed mowing the lawn.

MS. DOUGLAS:

Now this is her diary. She talks about personal problems with her family, but it doesn't have a happy ending.

JIMMY:

Hmmm. Does she talk much about boys?

MS. DOUGLAS:

She does talk about boys, but it's mostly about her family and the people she lives with.

JIMMY:

(*trying to act like an "intellectual"*) Well, I'll read it anyway. I might learn something from her.

NARRATOR:

I tried to act like I was much more mature than I was. Miz Douglas had seen this before, but either she was very good at pretending she didn't see it, or because I was so young I couldn't tell that she could see right through me.

JIMMY:

It's not a very big book is it?

MS. DOUGLAS:

I'm sure it will keep you as involved as Mister Tolkien.

JIMMY:

It's not about Hobbits is it?

MS. DOUGLAS:

No, there are no Hobbits in the book.

JIMMY:

(*suspiciously*) You sure?

MS. DOUGLAS:

Yes. I've read it a couple of times.

JIMMY:

Good. I think I want something a little more real. Why do you think he spent so much time talking about their hairy feet?

MS. DOUGLAS:

What?

JIMMY:

Tolkien spent a lot of time talking about Hobbit feet being hairy and stuff. He even named one family 'Proudfoot.' What was that all about?

MS. DOUGLAS:

(*laughing to herself.*) I don't know. (*Ms. Douglas goes to a book shelf, retrieves the book, and brings it back to the desk to check out.*) Here's the book.

NARRATOR:

The book had been through some hard times. It had been taped up--repaired--at least three times over the years.

JIMMY:

Okay, I'll check it out. Can I get something else, too?

MS. DOUGLAS:

We just got a book in about chess in the Soviet Union.

JIMMY:

I don't know...

MS. DOUGLAS:

There is a chapter devoted to Bobby Fisher.

JIMMY:

(*excited*) Yes, Yes, YES! I'll take it. Wait, (*Ms. Douglas turns to him*) Who's it by?

MS. DOUGLAS:

Anton Gregorovich.

JIMMY:

Oooohhhh, I'd love to read that.

MS. DOUGLAS:

You don't mind that he's kind of dry?

JIMMY:

He's one of the best chess players in the world.

MS. DOUGLAS:

I'll get it for you. (*Ms. Douglas retrieves it and completes the check-out procedure, handing Jimmy the two books.*)

JIMMY:

If I can learn everything in here (*Jimmy adds the books to his backpack, then points to his backpack*) I will completely stun my Grandpa.

(*Exit Jimmy.*)

NARRATOR:

I remember this, clear as a bell on a cold day: As I was leaving, I was thinking how light my backpack felt that day. It seems that every day after that, my backpack got heavier and heavier. At that time, I had no idea how heavy it really was.

(*Lights out*)

Clif Mc Crady

ACT I, SCENE 2

Lights up. The bedroom of a 13-year-old boy. You can clearly see that in some ways, he is still a little boy and in others, he is trying to transition to adulthood. There is a lamp next to the bed. There is a chess table set up near the bed. His backpack is in the middle of the bed.

NARRATOR:

Whenever my grandparents visited, my grandfather and I would play chess. And it seemed since I broke my leg the first time, they came over more often. I liked it, especially since all of my friends had to be home by six. Grandpa could stay later.

(Enter Jimmy on crutches. Jimmy gets a box filled with chess pieces out from under the bed and starts to set up the chessboard.)

NARRATOR:

I had five different chess sets by the time I was thirteen. My favorite set had pieces that actually looked like people. A chess set is a chess set. As long as it had thirty-two pieces it was fine. But this set, Grandpa and I picked up at a flea market for five dollars, the weekend before I broke my leg the first time.

JOAN TALBOT:

(*Offstage*) Jimmy, get ready for dinner.

JIMMY:

(*Calling back*) Just setting-up for when Grandpa comes over tonight.

JOAN TALBOT:

(*Offstage*) Well get ready. Dinner will be on the table in about fifteen minutes.

JIMMY:

(*Finishing setting-up the chess pieces*) Okay.

(*SFX: Knock on the door*)

JIMMY (*Continuing*):

Who is it?

GRANDPA:

(*Enter Grandpa.*) Are you ready to get trampled?

JIMMY:

I don't know, it took you over a hundred and twenty moves to beat me last time.

NARRATOR:

I loved my grandfather, I still do. He was one of those people that made a difference in the world. If he told you something, then you could believe it because it was true. He said that if someone can't trust what you say, then you shouldn't open your mouth. Grandpa was one of the kindest people you would ever meet, but he was also someone you didn't want to cross. This was the year when I learned about the two things he hated. Not just what they were, but why. Simple things that really didn't make a difference in the greater scheme of things, but they were things he hated.

GRANDPA:

Well, if I can't beat you in less than one hundred and twenty tonight, I might as well quit playing.

JIMMY:

Well if I can't keep you at the table that long, then you didn't teach me well enough.

(*Both laugh*)

JOAN TALBOT:

(*Offstage*) You coming out?

JIMMY:

COMING!

GRANDPA:

What are we having for dinner? It smells good.

JIMMY:

Mom bought a brand-new cookbook. She had some big, blackish-looking squash plant. She called it...some kind of '-plant'.

GRANDPA:

An eggplant?

JIMMY:

Yeah, that was it. It didn't look so good when she was cutting it up.

GRANDPA:

Just smile, thank her for cooking it and eat it. I've seen hungry people when I was in Europe.

JIMMY:

Hey, Grandpa...

GRANDPA:

Yes.

JIMMY:

What did you do during World War Two?

NARRATOR:

A simple question, or so I thought. He never really talked about it. Whenever he did, he always said something like, 'When I was in Europe.' He never really elaborated or went into detail.

JOAN TALBOT:

(Offstage) Hurry up!

GRANDPA:

We'll be right there, Joan. (turning back to Jimmy) Oh this and that, drove a jeep, tried to capture a bridge or two.

NARRATOR:

That's how he described his involvement in the Second World War, a war where millions of people died. 'This and that.' No big deal. 'Drove a jeep.' If I didn't know better, I would have thought my grandfather spent World War Two driving a jeep...over bridges. My thirteenth year was a year of change and learning, in more ways than I care to think about.

JIMMY:

Did you fight the Germans or Japanese?

GRANDPA:

(*Coldly.*) Germans.

JIMMY:

(*Reaching for his crutches*) I was in the school library today, and they didn't have any books about pilots in World War Two. They didn't even have books about the planes.

GRANDPA:

Why not?

JIMMY:

(*Moving towards the door*) I dunno. Probably because they're heavy. We don't have a lot of heavy books in the library. I wanted to read something about Uncle David or at least the kind of stuff he did.

GRANDPA:

Don't say 'stuff.'

JIMMY:

Huh?

GRANDPA:

Don't say 'stuff.'

JIMMY:

Why not?

GRANDPA:

It's 'lazy speech'. When you say something, SAY something. And when you say something, MEAN it. Otherwise, don't speak.

JIMMY:

Sorry.

GRANDPA:

Don't be sorry, just don't do it. It's like in chess, you don't say 'check'. if you don't have the king in check. You have to remember that your words have power.

JIMMY:

Sure.

GRANDPA:

In some tournaments if you say 'check' when it is not a check you could lose the game. One word could cost you everything!

JIMMY:

(*Thinking about what he said*) Uh, I wanted to read about what pilots did in the war.

GRANDPA:

Hmmm, we'll see about that. No books that are heavy? What kind of silly nonsense is that?

JIMMY:

Guess they figure kids won't read heavy books.

GRANDPA:

Humph.

(*Jimmy and Grandpa exit.*)

NARRATOR:

I found out at the end of the year that he called Miz Douglas and asked her for a list of books she would recommend about World War Two pilots. He asked her to research for him, and when I found out, I was amazed she did. Grandpa always said, never be afraid to ask for help. I found out as I grew up, that he spent a lot of money buying books for the school library.

(*Lights out*)

ACT I, Scene 3

Lights up. In Jimmy's Bedroom, Grandpa sits in a chair, Jimmy on his bed. The chess board is between them.

JIMMY:

Dang it. (*Jimmy lays his king piece down on the board.*)

GRANDPA:

You're getting better.

JIMMY:

Thanks, Grandpa. Why can't I beat you?

GRANDPA:

Have you been studying the books I brought you?

JIMMY:

Yes.

GRANDPA:

Then you will get better. You need to remember that each move you make changes the course of the game. You can either force me along a course of action, or I can force you. But when the other side doesn't see that force, it is easier for them to walk right into the trap.

JIMMY:

Why do you like chess so much?

GRANDPA:

Hmmm...memories really. When we were boys I used to play with my brother, Martin.

JIMMY:

I don't remember an Uncle Martin.

GRANDPA:

He died a long time ago.

JIMMY:

When?

GRANDPA:

(*Taking a deep breath*) June of 'forty-four, in France; it was a hard day.

JIMMY:

What happened?

GRANDPA:

(*Hemming and hawing*) Hmmm. Well. (*Looking around and spying the backpack*) You...uh...have homework to do. And you need to think about the future. It's a long story. I'll tell you later. (*Reaches for the backpack and gives it to Jimmy*) I'll be back Saturday, so you do your homework. Next time we play, I'll be white.

JIMMY:

Thanks, Grandpa. Good night.

GRANDPA:

Good night, Jimmy.

NARRATOR:

Grandpa never talked much about the war--not to anyone--although, every once in a while, when there was a family get-together, Grandpa and Uncle Dave would talk about the war. But they always stopped talking when any of us grandkids came around.

(*Jimmy opens his backpack and pulls out the two books he got from Ms. Douglas.*)

JIMMY:

Which book? Hmmm.

NARRATOR:

Books have always seemed so alive to me; not just a black ink on a page. It always seemed as if the author was talking to me. I even found myself, on occasion, talking to the book.

The best part about having the broken leg was all the time I spent in the library. It was that year when I decided that I would have my own library when I had my own house.

JIMMY:

Girls. I'll start with the diary. (*Jimmy starts to set up the pillows on his bed to read the worn copy of the diary.*)

(*Enter a bearded man dressed in dark wool suit.*)

GREGOROVICH:

(*In a Russian Accent*) What, you no want to read my book?

JIMMY:

I'll read it.

GREGOROVICH:

(*Moving to the chess board*) You must read my book. (*Sits down and starts to set up the pieces.*)

JIMMY:

I said I'd read it.

GREGOROVICH:

I will teach you things, to make you stronger player. Teach you to make your offense, defensive and your defense, offensive.

JIMMY:

I know you will, but I want to get this one started. (*Holds the Diary up toward Gregorovich*) It's a small book. It shouldn't take that much time. Your book (*Holds up the chess book*) is so much bigger, and heavier.

GREGOROVICH:

Very well, I will go...for now. But when your grandfather comes back on Saturday, you will lose another game.

JIMMY:

You don't know that.

GREGOROVICH:

(*Gets up*) I know you better than you know yourself. (*Turns towards the door*) You will lose. (*He leaves the room.*)

JIMMY:

Finally, some peace and quiet. (*Addressing the battered book*) Good evening, Anne. How are you?

(*Enter Anne. She remains standing by the door.*)

ANNE:

For now, I am well.

JIMMY:

The Diary of Anne Frank. (*Opens book somewhere in the middle. Anne crosses halfway into the room, towards Jimmy's bed.*)

ANNE:

Dear Kitty... (*Anne moves closer to Jimmy's bed.*)

JIMMY:

Dear Kitty? Dear Kitty! What the heck is this? Who calls anything 'Kitty', unless it's a cat?

ANNE:

It's what I decided to call my diary. 'Dear Kitty' sounds better than, 'Dear Diary'.

JIMMY:

Oh...like Miss Kitty from Gunsmoke...wonder if this Anne liked Cowboy shows?

(*Jimmy flips to a different part of the book.*)

ANNE:

I've reached a point where I hardly care whether I live or die.

JIMMY:

How old is this kid? Geesh, she could be a little happier, I think. (*Flips to a different section of the book.*)

ANNE:

Maybe it would be best if you start from the beginning. Have you ever heard the term, 'hostages'?

JIMMY:

Of course. I remember the Olympics.

ANNE:

(*Curious.*) What happened at the Olympics?

JIMMY:

They killed all those athletes.

ANNE:

Who killed them?

JIMMY:

Those terrorists. They kidnapped them, then blew 'em up in the helicopters.

ANNE:

How very strange.

JIMMY:

I don't know how someone could do that.

ANNE:

(*Moving over and sitting on the foot of Jimmy's bed.*) That was not the first time things like that happened.

NARRATOR:

As I started to read Anne's diary, I began to learn about the girl's life. She told me so many things that I didn't know. She made me curious about more than just her life. She made me wonder about the events of her time. I learned she was just about my age, in fact, almost the exact same age.

JIMMY:

I don't get it. Why did you have to leave your house?

ANNE:

Because I am a Jew.

JIMMY:

Jew? Humph! What does that mean?

NARRATOR:

I had never met a 'Jew'. I had heard of Jewish people, and I liked Jewish rye bread. And I vaguely remembered things about the Jewish religion from Sunday School, but having to leave your house just because you are a Jew? It made absolutely no sense to me.

ANNE:

(*To herself*) I went to a different school than a lot of the other kids. (*To Jimmy*) My father had our family leave Germany because we were Jews. So, we moved to Holland.

JIMMY:

What does that have to do with anything?

ANNE:

You are going to have to ask someone else because I don't know what it has to do with anything, either. I had friends who were Jews and friends who weren't.

NARRATOR:

I knew that my grandfather wouldn't tell me much of anything. He never talked about the war except to tell me he drove a jeep over bridges. There was only one person I could talk to about this. I closed the book *(Jimmy closes the book; exit Anne)* and set it on the chess table next to my bed *(Jimmy sets the book on the table.)*

JIMMY:

(To himself) Jew?

NARRATOR:

I laid in bed for at least an hour, thinking about that one word, what it meant, rolled it around in my mind. Then I turned off the light and went to sleep. (*Jimmy turns off the light next to the bed.*)

(*Lights out*)

Clif Mc Crady

ACT I, Scene 4

Lights up. Junior High School library. Ms. Douglas is shelving books.

(Enter Jimmy on crutches.)

JIMMY:

(Calling from across the room) Miz Douglas?

MS. DOUGLAS:

Yes, Jimmy.

JIMMY:

I started reading that book you gave me last night.

MS. DOUGLAS:

Which one?

                    JIMMY:

The one about Anne Frank.

                    MS. DOUGLAS:

Did you learn anything?

                    JIMMY:

Well...I was confused about something she said.

                    MS. DOUGLAS:

What was that?

                    JIMMY:

It said that her family had to move to Holland because they were Jews.

                    MS. DOUGLAS:

Yes?

                              JIMMY:

What does that mean?

                              MS. DOUGLAS:

What does what mean?

                              JIMMY:

What does she mean when she says, she's a 'Jew'?

                              MS. DOUGLAS:

Well, do you know any Jews?

                              JIMMY:

(*Thinking*) No...I don't. Miz Douglas, what does
it mean to be a Jew? To be Jewish?

                              MS. DOUGLAS:

Well...

JIMMY:

Anne said she had to leave her home in Germany because she was a Jew. What does that have to do with anything? I asked my mom about it and she said the Jewish religion was older than ours. (*suddenly has an idea*) Oh, and that they can't eat ham at Easter. (*thinking*) Why would you have to leave your house because you're Jewish? Are they allergic to ham?

NARRATOR:

I knew nothing. And it showed. How could you live your life in such a vacuum? How could you not know anything about one of the most important events in the last hundred years? Looking back, I think about how blissfully ignorant I was. But I wanted to know...

JIMMY:

What does it mean?

MS. DOUGLAS:

(*Trying to keep from laughing*) It is a little more complicated than the occasional ham sandwich.

JIMMY:

Why would you have to leave your house?

MS. DOUGLAS:

Jimmy, there is a lot more than just that. You are asking one simple question, but its answer is not that simple. What do you know about World War Two?

JIMMY:

Not a lot. I know that my grandpa--my dad's dad-- was there and so were two of his brothers. Oh, I just learned his brother, Martin, died in the war. I know that my grandmother's brother was a pilot. That's about it. Hmmm. Yep, that's about it. Oh, and I like watching 'Hogan's Heroes'.

(*Looking down*) I really don't know anything else. No one talks about the war, really.

MS. DOUGLAS:

Well, while you are in here for your hour each
day, you will help me work on a wall project
about World War Two, so that others can learn
what you are learning. How does that sound?

JIMMY:

Fair. It could be fun.

NARRATOR:

I had no idea what I was going to learn. I would
learn about the Eighth Air Force, I would learn
about Pearl Harbor, V-2 Rockets, D-Day. I would
learn about the invasion of Poland. Words would
enter my vocabulary that had never been there
before. 'Blitzkrieg'...'Bocage'...'Gestapo'...
'Bastogne'...'Vichy'. But I would learn so much
more. I would discover some family walls, and
eventually, I would break some down with
everything that that entails, both the good and
the bad.

MS. DOUGLAS:

Well, which wall should we work on and what
should we start with?

JIMMY:

My grandpa says you should always start at the
beginning. So, we should probably start at the
beginning.

MS. DOUGLAS:

Which beginning?

JIMMY:

(*Rolling his eyes*) The start of World War Two!

MS. DOUGLAS:

(*Knowingly*) When was that?

JIMMY:

Come on, everyone knows it was when the Japs
bombed Pearl Harbor.

MS. DOUGLAS:

You mean the Japanese?

JIMMY:

That's what I said.

MS. DOUGLAS:

No, you said 'Japs'.

JIMMY:

What's the difference?

MS. DOUGLAS:

Japanese people don't like to be called 'Japs'.
It is not a nice word to them.

JIMMY:

(*Confused*) It's not? Uh, sorry.

NARRATOR:

I would learn that names can be the beginning.
Once you get beyond thinking of others as people,

you could do all kinds of things to them. Another word entered my vocabulary: 'Untermenschen.' Oh, how I would learn about that word.

MS. DOUGLAS:

So, you think that the bombing of Pearl Harbor was the start of the war?

JIMMY:

Yep.

MS. DOUGLAS:

Okay. While you are in the library today, I want you to find out when World War Two started for Great Britain, France, China, Poland, the Soviet Union, and the United States.

JIMMY:

Uh, December seventh...when the Japanese bombed Pearl Harbor.

MS. DOUGLAS:

(*Rolling her eyes*) Please, humor me, Jimmy. Use the encyclopedia.

JIMMY:

Alright, but it's still going to be December seventh.

MS. DOUGLAS:

Maybe. We'll see.

(*Lights out*)

ACT I SCENE 5

Lights up. Jimmy's Room. Anne and Gregorovich are sitting on Jimmy's bed, each holding their respective book. Narrator stands near door to bedroom.

NARRATOR:

There they were, waiting patiently for my return--right where I left them. Each wanting my time and attention.

GREGOROVICH:

What do you think you can teach him?

ANNE:

I don't know. He'll have to figure that out for himself.

GREOGOROVICH:

Your's is sad story. Too much for young boy, I fear.

ANNE:

He and I are about the same age.

GREGOROVICH:

Da. But they were different times.

ANNE:

But they need to be remembered.

GREGOROVICH:

Why? So everyone can learn about killing and death and cruelty?

ANNE:

No, so they can learn FROM it. So they can learn...how to LIVE.

GREGOROVICH:

Chess will teach him to be responsible for his actions. Teach him to make good choices. To think. Young men need to learn to think for themselves, so don't become robots... or worse, slaves.

ANNE:

Why don't we let him decide which of us he would prefer?

NARRATOR:

I had left both books on my bed because I wanted to make sure I knew where each one was. Mom wasn't tough on me about making my bed since my leg was in the cast. It was one of the best things about having a broken leg. Well, that and the sympathy I got from some of the girls. Hannah Kirschbaum and Maria Machado would always help me sharpen pencils, turn papers in, that kind of thing. Both of them were very nice.

ANNE:

He wants to know what happened.

(*Enter Grandpa moving towards the chess board.*)

GREGOROVICH:

My game will keep the them together long after (*pointing at Grandpa*) he is gone. It may be only good memories they have.

GRANDPA:

(*Looking at the books on the bed, Grandpa picks up the diary.*) *The Diary of Anne Frank!* Oh my. I don't know if he is ready for this. (*Sits in his chair.*)

GREGOROVICH:

Do you see? Even his grandfather is not sure if he should learn about the horrors of that time.

ANNE:

If not now, when?

GRANDPA:

If not now, when? When do I tell him? (*pause*) *Do
I tell him? When should he learn?* (*Sits in his
chair with a distant look on his face.*) Martin,
when should he learn about it?

ANNE:

Do you see how much of his family this affects?
He is curious now, so now is when he should
learn.

GREGOROVICH:

I guess he can't be protected forever.

ANNE:

And he wants to know.

GRANDPA:

I guess if he wants to know, I should tell him.
It would be better than learning from some
pinhead who doesn't know from Shinola.

JOAN TALBOT:

(Offstage) Dad, you want to come out here and help me with these steaks?

GRANDPA:

Be right with you, Joan.

ANNE:

How are you going to tell him?

GRANDPA:

I have no idea how to tell him.

GREGOROVICH:

Tell him the facts.

ANNE:

Tell him the truth.

GRANDPA:

(*To himself*) Jimmy, my brother Martin and I were in the Army in World War Two. We both landed in Normandy on D-Day. Your uncle Martin was killed there. (*thinking*) No, that's too cold.

ANNE:

That is a little harsh.

GREGOROVICH:

It's the truth.

ANNE:

He could say it in a softer manner.

GREGOROVICH:

Why should he sugar-coat the truth?

ANNE:

It will still be the truth, it just won't be so...cold.

GREGOROVICH:

Maybe it would be easier on the grandfather to tell it more...distant?

GRANDPA:

I fought in France, Holland and Germany.

ANNE:

Simple facts.

GRANDPA:

I learned how cruel people can be. (*pause*) We liberated a Death Camp. (*starting to sob*) How do I tell my grandson about a Death Camp? (*picks up* The Diary of Anne Frank)

ANNE:

(*Moving towards Grandpa, comforting him*) Just tell him.

(*Grandpa exits.*)

NARRATOR:

Grandpa didn't tell me that night. He didn't stay for dinner, either. As a matter of fact, I think Grandpa stayed away from our house for about a month.

It was an eternity to me. He always had a good reason for not being there, but until I was an adult, I didn't fully realize what was going on.

(*Lights out*)

Clif Mc Crady

ACT I, Scene 6

Lights up. Junior High School library, Ms. Douglas is sitting at her desk. Enter Jimmy on crutches. He goes over to one of the tables and sets his backpack down.

JIMMY:

Miz Douglas...

MS. DOUGLAS:

Yes, Jimmy.

JIMMY:

I think I have a problem.

MS. DOUGLAS:

Alright, what is it?

JIMMY:

I don't know when it started.

NARRATOR:

This became a very upsetting point to me. I had always thought the war started on December seventh.

MS. DOUGLAS:

'A day that will live in infamy.'

JIMMY:

That's what President Roosevelt said. But was it the start? It was for America. But, each of those countries in their own way had their own start.

NARRATOR:

For me personally, it started on that winter day in the library, because until that day, I really didn't know anything about the war.

MS. DOUGLAS:

What do you mean?

JIMMY:

World War Two. It started before nineteen forty-
one in Poland and France. I was reading an
article in the encyclopedia and it said that the
Japs, err, ah, the Japanese invaded Manchuria in
the nineteen thirties.

(*Frustrated*) How are we supposed to know when it
started if no one agrees on any of this?

MS. DOUGLAS:

Jimmy, don't worry about that. All you need to do
is present the facts. Just tell the truth. So
many things are not black and white, there is a
lot of gray out there. The start of World War Two
is one of those gray facts.

NARRATOR:

I think this was when I started realizing that so
many things were gray.

JIMMY:

It's stupid.

MS. DOUGLAS:

It's life.

JIMMY:

It's confusing.

MS. DOUGLAS:

So, how do you think you want to explain to everyone about the start of the war?

JIMMY:

I guess (pause) we need to tell them when it started everywhere and then they will have to decide.

MS. DOUGLAS:

Just tell them the facts. Most kids are smart
enough to make up their own minds.

JIMMY:

That makes sense to me.

NARRATOR:

Just give them the facts, and then let them make
up their mind; it was a good life lesson. It was
also a life lesson that has served me well for
the rest of my life.

JIMMY:

Maybe we could make it a game?

MS. DOUGLAS:

What do you mean?

JIMMY:

Get everyone to guess the start of the war and
then the winner gets a prize. Could we do a
prize? (*Jimmy stands.*)

NARRATOR:

I had no idea she would buy the prize with her own money.

MS. DOUGLAS:

Sure, we could do a prize of some kind.

NARRATOR:

When all was said and done, I think she probably spent about eighty dollars of her own money. Now that doesn't seem like a lot, but librarians weren't paid that much back then, and the minimum wage was only about two dollars and thirty cents an hour. It was a huge hit to her available cash. She never complained.

MS. DOUGLAS:

Maybe pizza, as a prize?

NARRATOR:

It was a huge hit to her available cash. She never complained.

MS. DOUGLAS:

JIMMY:

That would be great! Everybody loves pizza! (*Jimmy walks to one of the tables and prepares to sit down.*)

MS. DOUGLAS:

I have some more items coming in next week you might want to look at.

JIMMY:

What kind of things?

MS. DOUGLAS:

I talked to some of the veterans at the V.F.W. to ask if they would be willing to share with us, for your project, about their World War Two experiences.

JIMMY:

That would be so cool.

MS. DOUGLAS:

They said that they had pictures, some souvenirs and other things. Also, a friend of mine from college works at the National Archives, and he is going to send us some old Army photos. Those might make your project more interesting.

JIMMY:

Oh, yeah! Those could be so neat. Do you know how many pictures?

MS. DOUGLAS:

He said the pictures were from a regimental photographer in the European Theatre. He said the collection will have between five hundred and a thousand.

JIMMY:

Wonder what we'll see.

MS. DOUGLAS:

I'm looking forward to seeing those pictures myself. My mother grew up in Europe.

NARRATOR:

According to my grandfather, he grew up in Europe, as well.

(*Lights out*)

Clif Mc Crady

ACT I, Scene 7

Lights up. In Jimmy's bedroom. He is sitting on the bed. The Diary of Anne Frank is next to him on the bed. Anne is sitting on the foot of the bed. It looks like Jimmy has been crying.

ANNE:

What's the matter?

JIMMY:

You die.

ANNE:

It happens.

JIMMY:

But, you die.

ANNE:

They were hard times. Millions of people died. Over one million children died. I was just one of them.

JIMMY:

(*Upset*) I'm reading this stupid book about you, but it doesn't end. And then, I find out that you die?

ANNE:

I wanted to be an author. This is my biggest work. I want people to read it, to be part of it. You did that!

JIMMY:

(*Angry*) It sucks. You were just a little older than me.

ANNE:

Where does it say I died?

JIMMY:

Here--in the appendix--in a place called Bergen-Belsen, a prison for women. (*Confused*) Wait. Not a prison, it was called a concentration camp.

(*Enter Gregorovich.*)

GREGOROVICH:

It was a Death Camp. They put people that were considered "less than human" in those camps.

JIMMY:

A Death Camp?

GREGOROVICH:

I liberated one of those camps. It was horrible. The bodies, the smell...

JIMMY:

How could they do that?

GREGOROVICH:

...the sickness.

ANNE:

I don't know.

GREGOROVICH:

It is chess. In chess, how important is a pawn?

JIMMY:

(*Turns to Gregorovich*) What?

GREGOROVICH:

When you play chess with your grandfather, you sacrifice your pawns. Why?

JIMMY:

They have no value?

GREGOROVICH:

Does your grandfather do that?

JIMMY:

No.

ANNE:

Because to him, they have value.

GREGOROVICH:

They *are* valuable.

JIMMY:

(*Throws the books on the floor*) They are *just* pawns.

GREGOROVICH:

And you are free to do with them what you will. You can sacrifice them if you want, and you do. But as you deplete that resource, your chance of victory goes down.

JIMMY:

But sometimes you have to sacrifice a piece.

GREGOROVICH:

But not all of them! When you can't think of what to do, you sacrifice a pawn.

ANNE:

Why do you do that?

GREGOROVICH:

How many games have you lost because you threw away one pawn?

JIMMY:

Look, a chess game is not a Death Camp.

GREGOROVICH:

Is same principle. You talk about pawns as if
they are inferior pieces.

JIMMY:

THEY ARE!

GREGOROVICH:

They have purpose! Each ONE of them!

JOAN TALBOT:

(*Offstage*) JIMMY!

JIMMY:

What?

JOAN TALBOT:

(*Offstage*) Get ready for dinner!

NARRATOR:

I couldn't eat. For about a week, I barely ate anything. I just couldn't, thinking about Anne. She dominated my thoughts. Almost all of them went to her.

JIMMY:

Not hungry.

JOAN TALBOT:

(*Offstage*) Are you sick?

JIMMY:

No.

JOAN TALBOT:

(*Offstage*) THEN, YOU NEED TO GET READY FOR DINNER!

JIMMY:

I'm *not* hungry!

JOAN TALBOT:

(*Offstage*) Hungry or not, you need to eat. So, get ready for dinner.

ANNE:

I had some problems with *my* mother.

JIMMY:

It's not the same.

ANNE:

Everyone has problems with their mother.

JIMMY:

My problems are different.

ANNE:

Different...just like everyone else.

NARRATOR:

It always seems different but so much is the same. Everyone has problems with their mothers. It's funny how much like them you become as you get older...it's even funnier how much you miss them when they are gone.

(*Lights out*)

ACT I, Scene 8

Lights up. Miz Douglas is sitting at her desk working on a report and listening to Beethoven.

(SFX: Beethoven's String Quartet opus 130 Cavatina.)

The phone on her desk rings.

MS. DOUGLAS:

(Turns down the music, answers the telephone) Central Junior High School library, Miz Douglas.

JOAN TALBOT:

(On the phone) Miz Douglas, this is Joan Talbot, Jimmy Talbot's mother. I spoke with the office and they suggested that I talk with you.

MS. DOUGLAS:

What about? How can I help?

JOAN TALBOT:

(*On the phone*) Jimmy has become rather withdrawn. He seems to be avoiding family...trying not to be around anyone. He seems to be much more moody.

MS. DOUGLAS:

Okay. What are you thinking?

JOAN TALBOT:

(*On the phone*) I have read all the pamphlets and we have some neighbor kids who are older than Jimmy, and well...

MS. DOUGLAS:

Jimmy is a good kid.

JOAN TALBOT:

(*On the phone; nervously*) Could...could it be drugs?

MS. DOUGLAS:

Drugs? Jimmy? No, I am pretty sure that he is not involved with drugs.

JOAN TALBOT:

(*On the phone*) What about marijuana?

MS. DOUGLAS:

I am pretty sure that he is not involved with drugs of any kind.

JOAN TALBOT:

(*On the phone*) But the mood swings?

MS. DOUGLAS:

Jimmy is in the library every morning during lunch for his P.E., and after school until someone comes to get him. Kids that do drugs don't come into the library on their own.

JOAN TALBOT:

(*On the phone*) Are you sure?

MS. DOUGLAS:

Oh yes, I am sure.

JOAN TALBOT:

(*On the phone*) But those older kids...

MS. DOUGLAS:

I will keep an extra watchful eye on Jimmy for you.

JOAN TALBOT:

(On the phone) Thank you. Mister Taylor said you would be so helpful.

MS. DOUGLAS:

Anything I can do to help.

JOAN TALBOT:

(*On the phone*) It's so hard nowadays to raise a good child.

MS. DOUGLAS:

You *did* raise a good child.

JOAN TALBOT:

(*On the phone*) Thank you. And thank you for your help. Good-bye.

MS. DOUGLAS:

Anytime, good-bye. (*Hangs up telephone*) Goodness sakes! (*Goes to shelve some books*) Well, at least she's paying attention.

(*Enter Jimmy*)

JIMMY:

Hello.

MS. DOUGLAS:

Hello, Jimmy.

JIMMY:

What, no music today?

MS. DOUGLAS:

I was listening to Beethoven, but the phone rang so I turned it down.

JIMMY:

You play Beethoven a lot.

MS. DOUGLAS:

My mother loves Beethoven. When she was younger she was in a small orchestra.

JIMMY:

That's cool.

MS. DOUGLAS:

She said that during the war, Beethoven kept her alive.

JIMMY:

Cool. My grandpa is coming to pick me up today. You should meet him.

MS. DOUGLAS:

I'd like that.

JIMMY:

He's the one that has been teaching me how to play chess.

MS. DOUGLAS:

He must be a very good player.

JIMMY:

He's the best. (*thinking*) Well, second best. His brother is the best. He was State Chess Champion when he was younger. Grandpa is always bragging about him.

MS. DOUGLAS:

I look forward to meeting him.

JIMMY:

Can I leave my backpack here, while I go to the restroom?

MS. DOUGLAS:

Sure. (*Jimmy turns to exit.*) Oh, Jimmy, this was delivered this morning. It's from the V.F.W.

JIMMY:

Bet it's got all the cool souvenirs in it. Can we look in it when I get back?

MS. DOUGLAS:

Sure thing! The man that delivered the box said there were even a couple of war diaries in it.

JIMMY:

Thanks. I'll be right back. (*Exit Jimmy. Ms.
Douglas turns the music back on. She then goes
back to her report.*)

(*Enter Grandpa. Ms. Douglas doesn't notice him.
He looks around the library. He notices the music
for moment he gets a far-away look in his eyes.*)

GRANDPA:

(*Clears his throat.*) Excuse me.

MS. DOUGLAS:

(*Turns around*) Yes, can I help you?

GRANDPA:

(*Obviously agitated*) I'm looking for my grandson,
Jim Talbot.

MS. DOUGLAS:

(*Crosses to Grandpa*) He'll be right back. He
stepped down the hall. I'm Linda Douglas, the
librarian. Jimmy's a great kid. (*extends her
hand*)

GRANDPA:

Thanks. (*Grandpa begins to reach for her hand but changes and puts it in his pocket. Ms. Douglas puts her hand down.*) The librarian?

MS. DOUGLAS:

Yes.

GRANDPA:

(*Angry*) I wish you wouldn't tell him about World War Two.

MS. DOUGLAS:

(*Confused*) I have only been answering his questions. He's doing research.

GRANDPA:

I spent three years in that...hell. I saw things no one should ever see. (*sternly*) And he doesn't need to know about it!

MS. DOUGLAS:

He will learn a lot more about it in high school. But right now, he is just curious. He said you fought in the war and he wants to know about you. He really admires you.

GRANDPA:

I was at D-Day. I am the only man from my landing craft that didn't die that day. I saw my friends killed on that beach.

MS. DOUGLAS:

Oh, my.

GRANDPA:

(*With a faraway look*) The murdering fire. (angry) Jimmy doesn't need to know about that.

MS. DOUGLAS:

He just has the...

GRANDPA:

I just want you to...

(*Enter Jimmy. He senses the tension.*)

NARRATOR:

I could tell Grandpa was mad. But I didn't know why.

JIMMY:

Grandpa, this is Ms. Douglas.

GRANDPA:

(*Coldly*) We've met.

MS. DOUGLAS:

Let me get you your pack Jimmy.

(*Ms. Douglas hands Jimmy his backpack.*)

JIMMY:

Thanks.

MS. DOUGLAS:

(*Hopeful*) Nice to meet you. (*Grandpa nods at Ms. Douglas.*) Good-bye.

JIMMY:

See you Monday.

(*Exit Jimmy and Grandpa*)

NARRATOR:

I had no idea what had happened. Ms. Douglas looked so sad when we left. Eventually, I learned about that meeting, what had transpired, and I understood, but what I really remember...is that it was a long, silent ride home.

(*Ms. Douglas crosses to her desk, puts her head in her hands and starts to cry.*)

(Lights out)

End of Act I

ACT II, Scene 1

At curtain rise, in Jimmy's Bedroom, Jimmy is sitting on his bed reading a book. Anne is sitting on the foot of the bed. Gregorovich is hovering around the chess board.

JIMMY:

Pawn to king's knight, four.

GREGOROVICH:

And now...

JIMMY:

and...

GREGOROVICH:

White moves bishop to queen's rook five.

JIMMY:

And then black moves king to king's rook three.

GREGOROVICH:

The Smolensk Gambit.

JIMMY:

Who moves their king that much? You should never have to move your king that much. (*looks at book*) What the heck is this guy thinking?

(*Enter Narrator.*)

GREGOROVICH:

You play with all the pieces.

JIMMY:

You can't do that!

NARRATOR:

My grandpa always told me that you only move the king when it is in trouble. Gregorovich was telling me that it was okay to move the king whenever I wanted.

GREGOROVICH:

You do what is unexpected.

JIMMY:

As long as it doesn't get you killed!

GREGOROVICH:

When you do what is unexpected, then your opponent will spend more time worrying about what other unexpected things you may do. Then you can do the more simple things with less trouble.

JIMMY:

Where's his protection? All he has by him is a couple of pawns.

GREGOROVICH:

If properly deployed, the pawns are all the protection he needs, the smallest can be powerful.

JIMMY:

No rooks! No knights!

GREGOROVICH:

All of the pieces! Nothing is held in reserve. You play with everything. You yield nothing.

(*Jimmy sets the book down. Looks at his chessboard and picks up a pawn.*)

GREGOROVICH:

You have question?

JIMMY:

This is the worst piece on the board, it can only move forward. Almost everything stops it.

GREGOROVICH:

Da!

JIMMY:

But just by making it across the board, it can become a queen.

GREGOROVICH:

Which means?

JIMMY:

The most...powerful piece on the board.

GREGOROVICH:

And that means what?

NARRATOR:

Every once in a while in your life, you have these moments of clarity. When everything seems to make sense. When you know, deep down inside, that what you are thinking is way beyond where you are. This was just such a moment to me.

JIMMY:

(*Pause*) No piece is insignificant.

GREGOROVICH:

Exactly!

JIMMY:

Every piece, no matter how small, can impact the entire game.

ANNE:

(*To herself*) I want to be a writer! I want to tell stories. I want people to know about...about us.

JIMMY:

So something that really doesn't mean that much, (*picks up* The Diary of Anne Frank) can become very powerful.

GREGOROVICH:

If you know how to use it.

JIMMY:

So a pawn becomes a queen.

GREGORVICH:

Da. Of course, if you do nothing with the queen, it still has the power to make your opponent think about what she *could* do. It makes your opponent fearful of certain moves.

JIMMY:

So, you just need to get it to the place...

GREGOROVICH:

...of transformation.

NARRATOR:

Transformation. Child to teenager. Teenager to adult. Writer to author. Chess player to chess master.

ANNE:

(To herself) The government wants us to document our lives so that others will know what we went through during the occupation.

GREGOROVICH:

And the pawn becomes a queen. (*points to Anne*)

JIMMY:

The most powerful piece on the board.

GREGOROVICH:

Remember that pawns are important.

JIMMY:

I see that.

GREGOROVICH:

Protect your pawns.

ANNE:

(To herself) I wonder if the government would even want my diary?

JIMMY:

(Picking up The Diary of Anne Frank*)* I wonder if she knew how powerful this would be?

NARRATOR:

I still wonder. What else could she have written that would have been as powerful as this one book. Could she have become that powerful in another time or place?

(Lights out)

ACT II, Scene 2

(Library lights at half. Ms. Douglas sits at her desk. Jimmy sits at a table reading a book. Across the table from Jimmy stands an SS Officer.)

(Lights to full on Jimmy and the SS Officer)

NARRATOR:

I found this book in the box from the V.F.W. It was a souvenir taken by one of the G.I.s off someone he either killed or captured. It, too, was unfinished. Whoever took it, translated it so you could see the German in the German's handwriting and the English in the American's handwriting. I was lucky that most of it had been translated already but some of the work hadn't been, so I would bring--sneak really--it into the library and translate some of the words myself. But at the time, I thought that Ms. Douglas wouldn't have liked the book if she had seen it. Not sure why, it was just a feeling.

DREIZINGER:

(*With a German accent*) So, what are you searching for?

JIMMY:

(*Looking at the book he is holding*) How could you do this?

DREIZINGER:

Answers. You want answers, ja?

JIMMY:

Yes, I have been reading about World War Two a lot lately, and I don't understand how you could do this.

DREIZINGER:

Do what?

JIMMY:

Treat people like this.

DREIZINGER:

Ah. You mean *untermenschen*.

JIMMY:

What is '*untermenschen*'?

DREIZINGER:

Lesser...people.

JIMMY:

Lesser people?

DREIZINGER

Not...quite...human.

JIMMY:

They look like you do...?

DREIZINGER:

(*Angry*) THEY DON'T LOOK ANYTHING LIKE ME! Look at their eyes. That nose. HOW DARE YOU THINK THOSE JEWS LOOK LIKE ME!

JIMMY:

They have two eyes. Look at this woman. She has pretty eyes.

DREIZINGER:

(*Begins to pace*) They are the eyes of a rat.

JIMMY:

What...

DREIZINGER:

Vermin!

JIMMY:

But...

DREIZINGER:

Let me explain this in terms you might better understand: Have you ever set a mouse trap?

JIMMY:

Yes.

DREIZINGER:

Why?

JIMMY:

To get rid of the mice, of course.

DREIZINGER:

Why do you want to 'get rid of the mice'?

JIMMY:

They'll take over and destroy the house. And they're gross.

DREIZINGER:

Why would you want to set a mouse trap? They are dirty, sometimes bloody, and sometimes the mouse gets away.

JIMMY:

But if the mice take over the house I can't live there anymore.

DREIZINGER:

(*Sits*) I think you are beginning to understand. That is where we were. Mice are vermin. You destroy them to protect yourself. The Jews...same thing!

JIMMY:

(*Stunned*) What?

DREIZINGER:

If we don't get rid of these...vermin...then they will destroy our house, our nation. They will breed with our children. They will sell us into slavery to the Bolsheviks. They have colonies in our country and you must destroy the rat's nest.

JIMMY:

But aren't they people?

DREIZINGER:

Why do you say this?

JIMMY:

(*Unsure of himself*) Because, I can see the pictures and they look like people you would see...anywhere.

DREIZINGER:

That is where you are wrong. Our scientists, our geneticists, our doctors have proven them to be *untermenschen*.

JIMMY:

Look here. (*points to a picture in the book*) This picture of a German soldier pushing around an old lady...how is she a threat?

DREIZINGER:

(*Slowly*) She breathes.

JIMMY:

That's crazy.

DREIZINGER:

(*Standing*) NEVER say that!

JIMMY:

But...

DREIZINGER:

(*Accusing*) You have been corrupted. Brainwashed. By their international conspiracy. They ruined Germany after the Great War. They took away land and gave it to the Communists. They bankrupted our nation. Have you any idea how hard it was to buy a loaf of bread? Our children were starving...because of them.

JIMMY:

No, they didn't. I read that book.

DREIZINGER:

(*looking at the bookshelf*) By Albert Goldstein. *Ja*, lies.

JIMMY:

They wouldn't put lies in the library.

DREIZINGER:

Lies.

JIMMY:

What about the concentration camps?

DREIZINGER:

Have you seen one?

JIMMY:

No.

DREIZINGER:

Hollywood. Hollywood makes up all kinds of things.

JIMMY:

What about the pictures?

DREIZINGER:

What pictures? These in the books?

JIMMY:

YES.

DREIZINGER:

Props. Fake photographs, made to make it easy for your army to come to kill us.

JIMMY:

I don't understand.

DREIZINGER:

Our nation began to prosper and *they* couldn't stand it.

JIMMY:

They? Who's 'they'?

DREIZINGER:

Our enemies.

JIMMY:

What enemies?

DREIZINGER:

Are you blind? When did the Fatherland not have enemies?

JIMMY:

But...

DREIZINGER:

Alright, I will explain. You are young and don't really know much and you have been taught so much bad information.

At the end of the Great War--World War One--our country, Germany, was betrayed. We should have been able to win that war. We had better soldiers, better equipment, and we were defending ourselves. France and Britain declared war on us.

DREIZINGER: (*Continuing*)

Who betrayed us? The Communists, Trades Unionists and the Jews betrayed us. They didn't fight, they held up production, they kept us from winning.

We were never defeated on the field.

Then there was that treaty. It crippled us. To buy a loaf of bread it would cost thousands of marks. That's our money. Because of the Jewish bankers our money was worth nothing. Our children were starving. Old ladies starving!

After the war was over, the French and Belgians occupied part of our country. Aided by the Jews!

(*With pride*) But then the Führer came. He gave us jobs, purpose. Men had pride. We could eat. We also learned why everyone hated us. It was because we are the Master Race, the people that everyone wishes they were. But only the very best could be. We were envied and that envy turned to hatred. So we had to defend ourselves, from our enemies inside the country and out.

The Führer showed us how the Bolsheviks wanted to destroy us because they were so envious of us.

And he told us--he *showed* us--how most people everywhere were ignorant of the whole Jewish conspiracy. That conspiracy would lead to not only our destruction, but to the ruin of our children. How could any person want their children to be destroyed?

Have you seen the proof that we are the superior race?

JIMMY:

No.

DREIZINGER:

Faulty education, only showing you one side.

JIMMY:

I don't get it.

DREIZINGER:

You are young. Of course, you don't understand. You shouldn't have to worry about this. Just know that other nations are jealous, and we need to defend ourselves. That is all you need to know about this.

JIMMY:

Look, I'm just thirteen, and even I can see that this is messed up.

DREIZINGER:

In the States you don't have enemies everywhere around you, invading you, attacking you, chewing on the lifeblood of your people, trying to dilute your race into some mongrel breed of misfits.

JIMMY:

But aren't people...just people?

DREIZINGER:

You have obviously been taught much bad information. (*sits*)

JIMMY:

(*Closing the book; lights to full*) Ms. Douglas, I just don't understand.

MS. DOUGLAS:

What don't you understand?

JIMMY:

The Germans.

MS. DOUGLAS:

People are people, and sometimes they can be led by the bad into thinking they are doing something good.

JIMMY:

What?

MS. DOUGLAS:

Germany was hijacked. When the Führer and his supporters came to power, people thought they had voted for work. They didn't realize a few here, few there, and before they knew it, millions of people would be dead.

JIMMY:

I've heard that a lot of false information was made up to justify the war...so we would go over there and fight.

MS. DOUGLAS:

Do you believe that?

JIMMY:

I don't know. All I have are these books.

MS. DOUGLAS:

(*To herself*) That's how it starts. (*To Jimmy*) You want to know if the books are accurate?

JIMMY:

I don't know why so many people would say it was
true if it wasn't. But I've heard that the
pictures were made up in Hollywood.

MS. DOUGLAS:

What do *you* think?

JIMMY:

But how do I know if they're real?

MS. DOUGLAS:

(*Sad*) You are going to have to make those
decisions for yourself. You've never met anyone
who lived in Germany during that time or a
survivor of one of those camps, someone who lived
in them, have you?

JIMMY:

No. I really never knew about any of this until
this year.

MS. DOUGLAS:

We are going to have to see what we can do about that.

JIMMY:

(*Somewhat sad*) How does such a thing happen?

MS. DOUGLAS:

Maybe it starts with a word or an action, or a lack of action.

JIMMY:

But if it is wrong, why would so many people do it?

MS. DOUGLAS:

People are still trying to figure that out.

NARRATOR:

'How does it happen?' To this day, that is a question I still can't answer. How many people around the world and over the years have been killed because they were labeled "*untermenschen*"?

(*Lights out*)

Clif Mc Crady

ACT II, Scene 3

(Jimmy's Bedroom. Grandpa and Jimmy sitting across the chess board. Anne is sitting by a window.)

JIMMY:

Grandpa.

GRANDPA:

(Studying the board) Yes.

JIMMY:

You said I could talk to you about anything...

ANNE:

I could talk to my father about anything...

GRANDPA:

(*Looks up at Jimmy, a smile across his face*)
Girls?

JIMMY:

Huh?

ANNE:

Every young boy wants to know about girls.

GREGOROVICH:

Girls will keep you from focus.

GRANDPA:

That little brunette, Maria? I've heard you talking with your friend, Dain, about her.

GREGOROVICH:

Maria. I have heard you talk about this girl. She keeps your focus off the board?

JIMMY:

Ummm... no. I've been working on a project at school.

GRANDPA:

Anything I can do to help your project?

JIMMY:

No, I want to know about World War Two.

GREGOROVICH:

Oh, now that's a tough question. (*To Grandpa*) Do you think he needs to know about this war, the death, the pain?

GRANDPA:

Oh, Jimmy, you really don't want to know about that.

GREGOROVICH:

(*To Grandpa*) You are not going to tell him this, are you?

JIMMY:

Yes, I do. I've been reading a lot about the war. There are some pictures they say I'm too young to see. Why?

GREGOROVICH:

You are too young! I was there. I fought that war. You don't want to know...

JIMMY:

I found out that Gregorovich even fought in the war. Did you know him?

GRANDPA:

There were a lot of people in that war. No, I didn't know Gregorovich. (*Grandpa gets up from chair and moves towards window.*) I guess you're going to find out sometime. I've thought about this for a while, how I would tell you.

ANNE:

He wants to know.

GRANDPA:

But are you ready?

ANNE:

He is ready.

JIMMY:

Just tell me.

NARRATOR:

I wasn't ready, yet I was. IF that makes any sense! I was ready to hear about it, but I wasn't ready to learn about it, because I had no idea...

GRANDPA:

(*Jimmy watches; Grandpa takes a deep breath.*) We all knew we would be going to war. We just didn't know when. My brothers, Martin and David, joined right after Pearl Harbor. I had to wait.

My mom and dad said they would give two sons, but not all three. That Sunday night, we drew straws and I lost. I had to stay. I wanted to go off on the 'Big Adventure'. I wanted to pay back those Japanese for what they did. What was funny is that I was drafted three months later. Dave's draft number never came up. If he hadn't volunteered, he would have been able to stay home. Will Gunther and I went in together. We did everything together. All the way until June of nineteen forty-four. (*Smirking*) The sergeant called us twins.

We spent months in England, waiting, training. (*reaches into his pocket and pulls out a coin*) The night before we left, Will gave me this coin. (*shows it to Jimmy*) That's it. Some photos, some memories. That's it. That's all I have to remember him by. When I die, who will remember Will? (*looks out the window*) Those days in England were great. Will had this English girlfriend, Marlene. She lived in London.

GRANDPA: (*continuing*)

In June of 'forty-four we invaded Europe. Martin dropped in behind the lines and died. I don't know if it was quick or if he suffered. I just don't know. I'll never know.

Will and I were on a landing craft. When it hit the beach and opened up, it was...it was the worst.

Will was in front of me. He was hit six times. I held him...he became a shield. He saved me. Only three of us that made it off that craft alive, and I am the only one that survived.

They are buried over in France. I miss both of them every single day.

JIMMY:

Uncle Martin and Will?

GRANDPA:

Yes, and a thousand other guys who didn't make it.

JIMMY:

What about the Jews?

GRANDPA:

No, I can't talk about that.

JIMMY:

I've been reading this book (*Jimmy picks up* The Diary of Anne Frank.) and her family had to hide. (*Anne turns towards Jimmy.*)

GRANDPA:

From the Nazis.

JIMMY:

I don't understand why.

ANNE:

Because we were Jews.

GRANDPA:

I learned a lot during my trip to Europe.

NARRATOR:

That's how Grandpa referred to his time in the Army: 'My trip to Europe.'

GRANDPA:

I don't know if I can explain this because I really don't understand it. The Jews worship the same God we do, they just do it differently. And in Germany, in those days, the Nazis had to make somebody the bad guy, so they picked the Jews.

JIMMY and ANNE:

Why?

GRANDPA:

Because there weren't a lot of them. and most people didn't care. Because they figured as long as the Nazis weren't bothering *them*, what's the harm? I heard some of the Germans say things like, 'I didn't know what the Nazis were doing.' or 'I thought it was just something between the Jews and Nazis.' But the Germans voted for Hitler. *They* voted for him.

JIMMY:

Hitler didn't like the Jews, so he had them killed?

ANNE:

I never knew him personally. What did I do to him?

JIMMY:

(*Holding up the book*) She was a kid, about my age. What did she do to him?

GRANDPA:

She breathed.

JIMMY:

That is what the German said.

GRANDPA:

What German?

JIMMY:

(*Grabs his backpack and pulls out the German diary. Enter Dreizinger.*) This one, *Helmut*

142

Dreizinger. He was an Ober...Oberführer in the SS.

GRANDPA:

The SS were some real bad guys. They killed lots of people.

JIMMY:

(*Nervously*) But you saved people?

GRANDPA:

(*Puts his head in hand, tears welling*) Not enough. We couldn't save enough.

NARRATOR:

I had never seen my grandfather cry. I didn't know he knew how.

GRANDPA:

I can still see the faces, the bodies...that slice of hell.

ANNE:

We were sent to a camp.

JIMMY:

I read about those...camps.

GRANDPA:

(*Wiping his eyes*) I saw one. I was there.

NARRATOR:

I was shocked. My Grandfather had actually seen one of those camps. When I read Dreizinger's book he called it a lie--a Hollywood fantasy. But my Grandfather was there. He *saw* it!

DREIZINGER:

(*Accusing towards Grandpa*) You lie.

GRANDPA:

The smell was horrible. There were people, my age...who looked like death. Rags hanging on their frames. (*Starting to sob*) And we were told we couldn't feed them. They were hungry, so damn hungry, and we couldn't feed them.

JIMMY:

How come?

GRANDPA:

Because the medics said it could kill them.

ANNE:

Disease was everywhere.

DREIZINGER:

They were diseased.

ANNE:

There was never enough to eat.

DREIZINGER:

They took the food from the mouths of German babies.

ANNE:

They shaved my head.

DREIZINGER:

We tried to clean them up.

ANNE:

People died every day. (*Crosses to Grandpa*)

DREIZINGER:

They used up our resources and gave us nothing!

GRANDPA:

When I was in Europe, we were sent to look for other camps. And we found one: It was a woman's camp. Each of those ladies looked like walking death.

After we liberated the camp, four of the women came up to us and started talking. I didn't speak

German. I had no idea what they were saying. It was all gibberish to me. One woman, she was wearing rags that bare covered her. She stank so bad. (*Choking back tears*) She had a small flower, she gave to me. I have kept that flower with me everywhere I go. (*Reaches for his wallet and takes out a small wax-paper envelope with a crushed, dried flower in it. He gets a far-away look in his eyes.*) I don't know what happened to her.

(*Focusing back on Jimmy*) Four of the ladies walked to one of the buildings and got musical instruments. These women, sick, hungry, and dirty, wanted to play us music. (*Choking up*) They were on death's doorstep, and they wanted to play *us* music. Music, in all that hell, just for us. I can't hear Beethoven without thinking of them, that camp, and the woman who gave me the flower. (*He shows Jimmy the flower.*)

One of the guys in my unit could speak German, and he told us some of what they were saying. Their children had been taken from them. A couple of months later, I was sent a photograph from the regimental photographer. He took a picture of the woman giving me the flower. He thought I would like to have it. I tore it up because you could see the hell this woman was living in and I didn't want to be reminded of it. I kept the flower because... (*Puts his head in his hands and sobs.*)

ANNE:

(*Sits down next to Grandpa*) You were able to save some people. I truly think that people are good at heart.

NARRATOR:

I was unable to say anything. I couldn't do anything. I was numb. (*Jimmy gets up and hobbles to Grandpa's side.*) My grandfather, the greatest man I knew, was brought to tears by remembering a woman he saw one time, thirty years ago. I will never forget the look on his face when he showed me that small flower.

GRANDPA:

(*Drying his eyes*) No one should ever see that. (*Anne crosses to window.*) Or live that. (*Angry*) Or *do* that to anyone else!

ANNE:

(*Looking out the window*) Whenever, I looked up at the sky, I felt that the cruelty would end, that peace would eventually return.

JIMMY:

(*Haltingly*) I guess that's what Ms. Douglas wanted me to learn.

GRANDPA:

She's a good teacher.

JIMMY:

But she's not a teacher, she's just a librarian.

GRANDPA:

No, Jimmy, she's a teacher. She's teaching you and, she's teaching me.

JIMMY:

Thanks for telling me. (*Gives Grandpa a hug.*)

GRANDPA:

It's hard Jimmy; remembering all those guys, what we saw. I just saw too much. (*Regains complete composure and stands up*) Now, you read some more, and go to sleep. You need your rest.

JIMMY:

Good night, Grandpa.

GRANDPA:

Good night, Jimmy. (*Exit Grandpa.*)

JIMMY:

(*Calling out*) Next time!

DREIZINGER:

You are seriously going to believe that?

JIMMY:

(*Picks up the German diary and puts it back in his backpack*) Yes. (*Exit Dreizinger.*)

NARRATOR:

At the beginning of the school year, I had no idea how much I was about to learn. After Grandpa told me his story, I thought I had learned too much. I was pretty sure that I had learned everything there was to learn. But it was a big war. Millions of people died, tens of millions suffered, hundreds of millions had their lives altered forever.

(*Crosses to Anne*) I'm glad I 'met' her, although I wish I hadn't. She became important to me from that time on. And yet, by the time I met her, she had been dead for over thirty years.

(*Lights out*)

Clif Mc Crady

ACT II, Scene 4

Jimmy and Grandpa are in the bedroom on opposite sides of the chess table. Gregorovich is pacing about the room. Narrator is by the window.

NARRATOR:

I started this evening's game, ready. I had finished the Gregorovich book, but kept it to go over some of his more complicated strategies. Tonight, I would beat my grandfather. I knew that *this* was the night.

JIMMY:

Check.

GREGOROVICH:

(*Surprised*) Excellent.

GRANDPA:

Are you sure you want to do this?

JIMMY:

Yep.

GRANDPA:

(*Captures the offending piece*) Checkmate.

JIMMY AND GREGOROVICH:

(*Surprised*) What?

GRANDPA:

Checkmate!

JIMMY:

But I was...

GRANDPA:

...doing a really good job.

JIMMY:

But why didn't I...

GRANDPA:

Win? Because I could see what you were doing.

JIMMY:

But...

GRANDPA:

Reading a book (*Picks up the Gregorovich book*) is good, but you need to remember that I can read it, too. He's good, this Gregorovich.

GREGOROVICH:

Thank you.

JIMMY:

He's one of the best.

GREGOROVICH:

I am a Grand Master.

GRANDPA:

You can learn a lot from him, but you need to learn to think for yourself. Never just follow someone's lead because you think they are smarter than you.

JIMMY:

What do you mean?

GRANDPA:

Don't always assume that someone is right just because they are smarter than you or bigger than you or because they are in charge. You need to think for yourself. Sometimes you need to stand up for something even when everyone else is against you.

JIMMY:

I think I get it.

GRANDPA:

(*Looking at the board*) You've changed some of your style.

JIMMY:

I have?

GRANDPA:

You seem to be respecting your pieces more.

JIMMY:

I think I've learned a lot.

GRANDPA and GREGOROVICH:

You have.

JIMMY:

Grandpa, I've been working on this World War Two project at school and I was wondering if you would come and take a look at it. See if I'm telling the story right.

GRANDPA:

I would love to. Where is it at? Is it in your homeroom?

JIMMY:

No.

GRANDPA:

Where is it?

JIMMY:

It's in the library.

GRANDPA:

Oh?!

JIMMY:

What's the matter?

GRANDPA:

I think your librarian is going to teach me another lesson.

JIMMY:

Huh?

NARRATOR:

I had no idea what had happened between my grandfather and Ms. Douglas, but I figured it was just a grown-up thing. I really just wanted him to see what I had been working on. It seems kind of funny, but I wanted his approval more than anyone else's. His opinion mattered so much more to me than almost everything else.

JIMMY:

Please come and see it.

GRANDPA:

Why don't I come in and see it when I pick you up tomorrow?

JIMMY:

That would be great.

(*Lights out*)

ACT II, Scene 5

In the library. Ms. Douglas is sitting at her desk. Enter Grandpa carrying a book wrapped in butcher paper.

GRANDPA:

Ms. Douglas.

MS. DOUGLAS:

(*Apprehensive*) Yes.

GRANDPA:

(*Standing straight*) I need to apologize to you.

MS. DOUGLAS:

(*Coyly*) Why.

GRANDPA:

I lost my temper the other day and you were the recipient. I shouldn't have done that.

MS. DOUGLAS:

That's alright. Things happen.

GRANDPA:

It is just that my grandson Jim has started to ask questions...

MS. DOUGLAS:

Yes...

GRANDPA:

The Second World War was difficult for me. I lost friends...and family.

MS. DOUGLAS:

Jimmy mentioned an uncle in the war who was a pilot?

GRANDPA:

His great uncle. (*giving her the book*) He flew B-17s over Germany.

MS. DOUGLAS:

(*Almost to herself*) Oh, my...What's this?

GRANDPA:

Jimmy said you didn't have any books on pilots during the war. This should make up for that.

MS. DOUGLAS:

(*Opening the package*) Thank you.

GRANDPA:

His plane went down.

MS. DOUGLAS:

I'm so sorry.

GRANDPA:

He survived and was captured.

MS. DOUGLAS:

Did he come home?

GRANDPA:

When he came home, he wasn't the same. (*choking back tears*) I can still see the old twinkle in his eye--how he used to laugh--before the war. He doesn't laugh any more. Jimmy reminds me so much of who he used to be. He was more than a brother. He was one of my best friends.

MS. DOUGLAS:

Goodness.

GRANDPA:

Jimmy lost his other grandfather to the Nazis. His great uncle, my brother Martin, died on D-day. I liberated one of those death camps. It was so horrible. I didn't think Jimmy needed to know any of this.

MS. DOUGLAS:

(*apologizing*) I never asked him to learn about his family. He was curious, so I just pointed him in the direction...

GRANDPA:

I know, it's not your fault. He's a smart kid. Eventually he'd learn about it. But...I just thought he was too young.

MS. DOUGLAS:

How old is Jimmy now?

GRANDPA:

Thirteen.

MS. DOUGLAS:

You know, when a Jewish boy turns thirteen he has a Bar Mitzvah.

GRANDPA:

We're not Jewish.

MS. DOUGLAS:

It is a kind of a coming of age ceremony, where the young man becomes responsible for so many aspects of his life. Maybe Jimmy is learning about this now, because he needs to become aware of what his family fought for, for the freedoms you and I share. Maybe, just maybe, this is Jimmy's equivalent of a Bar Mitzvah?

GRANDPA:

I'll think about it.

MS. DOUGLAS:

I've seen a lot of kids come in and out of this school over the last six years. Jimmy's a good kid. He was raised to be a good person.

GRANDPA:

Thank you.

MS. DOUGLAS:

It has a lot to do with you. Grandparents help kids find the right course in life.

GRANDPA:

Yours must have been good people.

MS. DOUGLAS:

I never knew my grandparents.

GRANDPA:

I'm sorry. (*a long pause*) May I show you something?

MS. DOUGLAS:

Of course.

GRANDPA:

When we liberated that camp, one of the ladies gave me this (*reaches into his wallet to pull out the flower and shows it to Ms. Douglas*).

MS. DOUGLAS:

What is it?

GRANDPA:

A little flower. This woman in rags gave this to me when we liberated the camp. They had nothing, and she found this to give to me.

MS. DOUGLAS:

(*confused*) She gave you this...flower...in the camp?

GRANDPA:

Yes.

MS. DOUGLAS:

This...reminds me of...excuse me a moment. (*She goes to a file with large 11x17 pictures in it, and pulls out a picture.*) I think (*looks back and forth between Grandpa and photograph*) this is you.

GRANDPA:

(*Looks at the picture*) Oh my...That's...me. This is the picture the photographer took. We moved out the next day. (long pause) I don't know what happened to her.

MS. DOUGLAS:

(*haltingly*) Would...you like...to know?

GRANDPA:

More than anything.

MS. DOUGLAS:

Excuse me a moment. (*goes to the door to the back room in the library*)

GRANDPA:

(*confused*) Huh?

MS. DOUGLAS:

(*calls back to him*) I'll be just a moment. (*Exit Ms. Douglas.*)

(*Grandpa gets a far-away look in his eyes as he studies the picture.*)

(*Enter Ms. Douglas and Sarah Stein.*)

MS. DOUGLAS:

Mr. Talbot, may I introduce you to my mother, Sarah Stein?

GRANDPA:

(*Looks at her*) I...

SARAH STEIN:

(*Looks at him*) My angel...

(*All action on stage freezes, except for the Narrator.*)

NARRATOR:

Ms. Douglas had arranged for me to meet a survivor, but how could I know who she was? My grandfather told me that he could tell it was her the moment he saw her. When he told me about meeting her, he kept saying she was healthy. Over and over. Healthy. My grandfather, haunted by those memories from so long ago, was able to find some comfort in the knowledge that she had survived and was healthy. They talked for hours. It was like two old friends seeing each other for the first time, reacquainting after a long absence. From then on, my grandparents and the Steins were seldom apart.

(Lights out)

ACT II, Scene 6

In the library, Sarah Stein sits at a table with Grandpa. Ms. Douglas is in the room, trying to do busy work and trying to pay attention to Sarah and Grandpa.

GRANDPA:

Tell me about your life. I need to know everything.

SARAH STEIN:

After the war, I lived in a Red Cross Refugee Center. It was nicer, cleaner than the camp. I spent so much time looking for my family. But they were all killed. My parents, aunts, uncles, grandparents, brothers, my sister, nieces, nephews...all gone.

GRANDPA:

How did you get here?

SARAH STEIN:

I met a soldier--an American soldier stationed in Germany. It was love at first sight. He came from Connecticut. He was a Methodist. He was at the checkpoint I had to pass every day. It was always a special treat to see him. We would talk, and talking led to walking. He was so alive. Then on one of our walks, I told him about the camp. He didn't care where I had been. He said he wanted to be with me where ever I go. I told him about my family. He offered me his.

I told him I would not marry a man who wasn't Jewish. I told him we would not be destroyed. And then he asked me a question, one little question: "Aren't we just people?" I started to cry. Yes, we were 'just people', and he didn't care about anything but me. Not what I had been through-- just me. We walked back. And he made a date to see me. We were going to a restaurant on Hilgertstrasse. When I got there, sitting next to him was an Army Officer. I found out it was a chaplain. So we spent the rest of the night trying to decide if he should become Jewish just to marry me.

SARAH STEIN: (*continuing*)

I spent the ten years before that, upset that I was a Jew. And here was a man who loved me so much that he would become Jewish for me. How could I say no?

I told him I wanted lots of children. No Hitler was going to destroy my family. And we had six beautiful children. My oldest son, we named Talbot, because of you. If you hadn't saved me that day, I would just be another body in a pit-- another casualty of the war. Because of you, I survived and I have six beautiful children and eleven grandchildren. (*looking at Ms. Douglas*) Could be more if my daughter would get to work. (*Both laugh.*) I couldn't ask for a better life. (*very serious*) Hitler did *not* win.

GRANDPA:

I haven't been able to get the image of that SS man's eyes out of my head all these years. I wasn't twenty feet away from that guard when I killed him. He changed me.

SARAH STEIN:

That's the difference between you and that man-- that guard. He would come into the camp eating a sandwich. We were starving to death and he would come in eating.

Then he would take the crust of his sandwich and throw it in the mud. The girls would fight for his leavings...to eat that dirty crust of bread. For him, it was great sport.

He killed because to him it was fun.

Wilhelmina Brauner was in one of those fights for the crust of bread and (*starts to tear up*) she broke her arm. He shot her in the head, because she couldn't work. (*regainint her composure*) I saw him kill her just because she was injured. He never cared about any of us.

GRANDPA:

Oh my God!

SARAH STEIN:

You saved us from him. He killed Silke Bahnhof, Anna Wolff, Eva Baum right in front of me. Ilse Silbermann, Heidi Grunwald, Eva Gottleib, Hannah Tischer and me...we were next. You gave us our lives back. Until you, we were dead.

GRANDPA:

If I had been faster, then those three wouldn't have died.

SARAH STEIN:

If not for you, there would have been nine dead.
And he might have gotten away.

GRANDPA:

But he changed me. In England, we sit around
talking about 'killing Nazis'. 'Gonna get me some
souvenirs'. That was all of us. We were on a
great adventure. When we landed on that beach,
things changed. When we fired our weapons we
aimed at shapes and in general areas. They can
train you, teach you how to kill, but when you do
it up close, something dies.

SARAH STEIN:

(*reaching out and putting her hand his*) That part
of you died, so we could live.

GRANDPA:

(*pulling his hand away*) But...

SARAH STEIN:

No buts. You can't have second thoughts. Those thoughts will never change.

GRANDPA:

(looking into her eyes) They changed me.

SARAH STEIN:

It changed all of us.

GRANDPA:

But I don't know if I'm a better man.

SARAH STEIN:

(grabs Grandpa's hand) You will always be a good man.

GRANDPA:

But I killed...

SARAH STEIN:

For life.

(Lights out)

Clif Mc Crady

ACTII, Scene 7

In the library. Sarah Stein sits at a table with Jimmy. Anne sits next to her. Dreizinger stands at the end of the table.

NARRATOR:

I spent the next several afternoons with Mrs. Stein. She told me things about the war--about the Nazis, about those camps--that I never could have learned anywhere else.

SARAH STEIN:

Any other questions?

JIMMY:

Sure, but I can't think of them right now.

SARAH STEIN:

I am lucky. Not many young people want to know about this history. They say it is too ugly.

JIMMY:

I really didn't want to know either.

SARAH STEIN:

Then why?

JIMMY:

(looks down) Because I wanted to know about girls.

SARAH STEIN:

What is wrong with that? Did you learn anything?

JIMMY:

I did.

SARAH STEIN:

You will need to remember this--what you learned.

JIMMY:

I don't think I will ever forget.

SARAH STEIN:

I have one more thing to show you.

JIMMY:

What's that?

SARAH STEIN:

This. (*She rolls up her long-sleeve shirt and shows a series of numbers on her arm.*)

JIMMY:

Why would you get a tattoo?

SARAH STEIN:

It was not my choice. Each of us were numbered.

ANNE:

Everyone in the camps were numbered; most were tattooed.

DREIZINGER:

So we could identify them better.

ANNE:

So they could control us better.

SARAH STEIN:

There were so many that didn't live.

JIMMY:

In some of the books I've been reading, there are people who say that there weren't camps. They say it didn't happen. I don't understand. I've seen the pictures. I read Anne Frank's diary. Why would someone say that it was all made up, that it wasn't real?

SARAH STEIN:

Because they don't want to remember what was done, or they feel guilty, or they don't care.

JIMMY:

But it's in the books. We'll remember.

SARAH STEIN:

Books burn.

NARRATOR:

I guess I had one more lesson to learn about this period of time. Those words, 'Books Burn', seemed to cut my heart out. To me, books are alive. When I read a book it is as if, the author is sitting there with me, talking to me. I know they aren't, but their words seem alive to me. The idea of burning a book was like burning a person.

SARAH STEIN:

We who are Jewish need to remember this.

JIMMY:

I'm not Jewish.

SARAH STEIN:

For this, you are Jewish enough. When I die, who will remember this camp? Who will remember Ilse Silbermann, Heidi Grunwald, Eva Gottleib, Hannah Tischer, and the others? Who will remember what your grandfather did...the lives he saved?

JIMMY:

I will. (*looks in Sarah Stein's eyes*) I'll remember for you.

SARAH STEIN:

Who will remember after you?

NARRATOR:

Another burning set of words: 'Who will remember after you?' I didn't know how to answer that question. I just sat there like a dumb thirteen-year-old kid, unable to think beyond the next weekend. I could only hope that I could someday, share what I had learned.

SARAH STEIN:

Too much for you, I know. But, God forbid, I die tomorrow, others need to know about this.

NARRATOR:

I said the only thing I could think of at the time.

JIMMY:

I'll make sure someone else remembers.

SARAH STEIN:

That's all I can ask.

JIMMY:

Mrs. Stein, I feel kind of bad about this.

SARAH STEIN:

What?

                        JIMMY:

I think I'm in trouble.

                        SARAH STEIN:

What did you do?

                        JIMMY:

I found this in a box of war souvenirs. (*reaches
into his backpack and pulls out the german diary*)

                        SARAH STEIN:

What's this?

                        JIMMY:

Well...an...SS man's diary.

                        SARAH STEIN:

What did you learn?

JIMMY:

That I don't understand them.

SARAH STEIN:

May I?

DREIZINGER:

DON'T LET HER TOUCH IT.

JIMMY:

Here. (*hands the diary to Sarah Stein.*)

SARAH STEIN:

(*Thumbs through the diary*) Goodness.

JIMMY:

What is it?

SARAH STEIN:

His own words about us. Names. Dates. Numbers.

JIMMY:

They're not nice.

SARAH STEIN:

So what are you going to do with this? *(gives the book back to Jimmy)*

JIMMY:

I wanted to destroy it...but I can't.

DREIZINGER:

Maybe there's hope...

SARAH STEIN:

I think others need to read this as well. May I give it to them?

DREIZINGER:

Do NOT let her keep that!

JIMMY:

Well...

SARAH STEIN:

I know some people who need to see this.

DREIZINGER:

NO!

JIMMY:

It's not mine, so you keep it. (*hands the book back to Sarah Stein.*)

DREIZINGER:

YOU FOOL! (*Exit Dreizinger.*)

(Lights out)

Clif Mc Crady

EPILOGUE:

Lisa sits in a chair, reading the book. On stage,
Narrator, center stage, holds a beat-up copy of
Anne Frank's diary. All dark, except Lisa and
Narrator.

NARRATOR:

I don't know if I have done a good job, telling
you about my thirteenth year. It was not my best
year--broken legs, illness--but I was able to
travel the world through the books in the
library. And Ms. Douglas, wherever she is now,
changed my world.

My Grandfather and I became closer than I could
have imagined. We talked almost every week when I
went off to college. He was my biggest supporter.

And when he died, just after graduation, I was
amazed at the number of people who turned out for
his funeral. Mrs. Stein and her husband were
there, and all six of her kids and twenty-two
grandkids.

And when Mrs. Stein died, I was at her funeral. And I thought that all those memories were gone, but I...will...remember. That was the last time I saw Ms. Douglas. She moved away and my family lost contact with her. (*Enter Anne. She crosses to Narrator.*) As I promised, I will continue to tell this story.

ANNE:

And I will continue to tell *my* story.

NARRATOR:

Her, with her words, and me with my grandfather's and Mrs. Stein's.

ANNE:

And yours?

NARRATOR:

(*looking at Anne*) And my words, too.

ANNE:

It's the only thing we can do.

NARRATOR:

(*Narrator and Anne walk over to Lisa. He reaches into the box and produces a little wax paper envelope and shows it to Anne, then turns to Lisa.*) Carry this flower to remind you about your great grandfather and Sarah Stein.

The things he did, the people he saved. Remember the people she lost.

Do this to remember them. (*Narrator offers Lisa the wax paper envelope. Lisa slowly closes the book and sets it down, and reaches for the wax paper envelope.*) Will you remember them?

LISA:

(*Takes the wax paper envelope*) Yes, Dad, I'll remember. (*a pause*) No. (*another pause; places hand on her stomach*) We'll remember.

(Lights out)

End of Act II/Play

About the Author

Clif Mc Crady is a graduate from California State University, Sacramento, with a bachelors in government, after which he worked for members of the California State Legislature and later the United States Congress. He moved to Wyoming in 1993 to care for an ailing grandmother and has since worked with people who are unemployed and/or living in poverty, teaching workshops on resume building, job searching, financial literacy, self-esteem, and other humanistic topics as needed. He has been involved in community theatre since 2003, playing Prince Barren in "Flash Gordon," Senior Chapuys in "A Man for All Seasons," directing "Romantic Comedy," "Miracle on 34th Street," and "My Three Angels." I'LL REMEMBER is his first screenplay-novel, based on a locally successfully produced screenplay he wrote of the same name.

I'll Remember

If you enjoyed *I'll Remember*, consider these other fine books from Aignos Publishing

The Dark Side of Sunshine by Paul Guzzo
Happy that it's Not True by Carlos Aleman
Cazadores de Libros Perdidos by German William Cabasssa Barber [Spanish]
The Desert and the City by Derek Bickerton
The Overnight Family Man by Paul Guzzo
There is No Cholera in Zimbabwe by Zachary M. Oliver
John Doe by Buz Sawyers
The Piano Tuner's Wife by Jean Yamasaki Toyama
Nuno by Carlos Aleman
An Aura of Greatness: Reflections on Governor John A. Burns by Brendan P. Burns
Polonio Pass by Doc Krinberg
Iwana by Alvaro Leiva
University and King by Jeffrey Ryan Long
The Surreal Adventures of Dr. Mingus by Jesus Richard Felix Rodriguez
Letters by Buz Sawyers
In the Heart of the Country by Derek Bickerton
El Camino De Regreso by Maricruz Acuna [Spanish]
Diego in Two Places by Carlos Aleman
Prepositions by Jean Yamasaki Toyama
Deep Slumber of Dogs by Doc Krinberg
Saddam's Parrot by Jim Currie
Beneath Them by Natalie Roers
Chang the Magic Cat by A. G. Hayes (a screenplay-novel)
Illegal by E. M. Duesel
Island Wildlife: Exiles, Expats and Exotic Others by Robert Friedman
The Winter Spider by Doc Krinberg
The Princess in My Head by J. G. Matheny (a screenplay-novel)
Comic Crusaders by Richard Rose (a screenplay-novel)

Coming Soon:
The City and the Desert by Derek Bickerton

Aignos Publishing | an imprint of Savant Books and Publications at
www.savantbooksandpublications.com

as well as these other fine books from Savant Books and Publications:

Essay, Essay, Essay by Yasuo Kobachi
Aloha from Coffee Island by Walter Miyanari
Footprints, Smiles and Little White Lies by Daniel S. Janik
The Illustrated Middle Earth by Daniel S. Janik
Last and Final Harvest by Daniel S. Janik
A Whale's Tale by Daniel S. Janik
Tropic of California by R. Page Kaufman
Tropic of California (the companion music CD) by R. Page Kaufman
The Village Curtain by Tony Tame
Dare to Love in Oz by William Maltese
The Interzone by Tatsuyuki Kobayashi
Today I Am a Man by Larry Rodness
The Bahrain Conspiracy by Bentley Gates
Called Home by Gloria Schumann
Kanaka Blues by Mike Farris
First Breath edited by Z. M. Oliver
Poor Rich by Jean Blasiar
The Jumper Chronicles by W. C. Peever
William Maltese's Flicker by William Maltese
My Unborn Child by Orest Stocco
Last Song of the Whales by Four Arrows
Perilous Panacea by Ronald Klueh
Falling but Fulfilled by Zachary M. Oliver
Mythical Voyage by Robin Ymer
Hello, Norma Jean by Sue Dolleris
Richer by Jean Blasiar
Manifest Intent by Mike Farris
Charlie No Face by David B. Seaburn
Number One Bestseller by Brian Morley
My Two Wives and Three Husbands by S. Stanley Gordon
In Dire Straits by Jim Currie
Wretched Land by Mila Komarnisky
Chan Kim by Ilan Herman
Who's Killing All the Lawyers? by A. G. Hayes
Ammon's Horn by G. Amati
Wavelengths edited by Zachary M. Oliver
Almost Paradise by Laurie Hanan
Communion by Jean Blasiar and Jonathan Marcantoni
The Oil Man by Leon Puissegur
Random Views of Asia from the Mid-Pacific by William E. Sharp
The Isla Vista Crucible by Reilly Ridgell
Blood Money by Scott Mastro
In the Himalayan Nights by Anoop Chandola
On My Behalf by Helen Doan
Traveler's Rest by Jonathan Marcantoni
Keys in the River by Tendai Mwanaka
Chimney Bluffs by David B. Seaburn
The Loons by Sue Dolleris
Light Surfer by David Allan Williams
The Judas List by A. G. Hayes

I'll Remember